A
Summer
Like
Turnips

LouAnn Gaeddert

❧ ❧ ❧

A Summer Like Turnips

Henry Holt and Company · New York

Published by Henry Holt and Company, Inc.,
115 West 18th Street, New York, New York 10011.
Published in Canada by Fitzhenry & Whiteside Limited,
195 Allstate Parkway, Markham, Ontario L3R 4T8.

Library of Congress Cataloging-in-Publication Data
Gaeddert, LouAnn Biegge.
A summer like turnips / by LouAnn Gaeddert. — 1st ed.
p. cm.
Summary: While spending his summer vacation at his grandfather's
retirement village, Bruce helps Gramps get over the recent death of
his wife.
ISBN 0-8050-0839-X
[1. Grandfathers—Fiction. 2. Death—Fiction. 3. Old age—
Fiction.] I. Title.
PZ7.G118Su 1989
[Fic]—dc19   88-37380

Henry Holt books are available at special discounts
for bulk purchases for sales promotions, premiums,
fund-raising, or educational use. Special editions
or book excerpts can also be created to specification.

For details contact:

Special Sales Director
Henry Holt and Company, Inc.
115 West 18th Street
New York, New York 10011

First Edition
Designed by Victoria Hartman
Printed in the United States of America
1 3 5 7 9 10 8 6 4 2

For Lucy and Louis

A
Summer
Like
Turnips

❧ 1 ❧

Bruce Hardy ran down the ramp from the plane, his tennis racket on his shoulder, a flight bag in his hand. This summer was going to be even better than other summers he had spent with Gramps. This summer was going to be as smooth and as sweet as a milk shake.

At the end of the ramp he searched the crowd of eager faces waiting behind the rope. Gramps was so tall, he would stand out in a crowd; not this crowd. Where was he?

Just for a minute Bruce's breath caught in his throat. Then he remembered—Gramps never could stand crowds. He probably thought Bruce was old enough now to make it to the baggage area on his own.

Bruce shifted his racket and pushed his way through the crowd. He stopped and stared at a man who looked like Gramps, only smaller and shaggier. The Gramps Bruce expected to see would be standing tall, searching for Bruce; this Gramps was leaning against a post, his head bowed.

Bruce bit his lip. Then he took a deep breath, pasted a smile on his face and called out, "Hey, Good Buddy."

Gramps' head jerked up on his skinny neck. "Hello, Bruce," he whispered. Last year he'd grabbed Bruce in a huge bear hug and thumped the air right out of his lungs. This time he didn't even shake his hand. "Let's get out of here."

"I have two more bags coming in on the lower level."

"More bags?" Gramps looked confused.

Bruce was confused too. Was it so unusual for a kid planning to spend a whole summer to have more than just a flight bag?

Gramps didn't say a word while they were waiting for the bags at the carousel. He didn't ask about the flight or things at home or Mom, his only daughter. He just stood there as if he were waiting for someone to tell him what to do next. Bruce wanted to snap his fingers in front of the old man's face.

"There they are," Bruce said as his bags came tumbling out of the chute.

Gramps didn't move, so Bruce stepped forward and pulled one bag from the carousel. He took it to his grandfather, then went back for the other.

For a minute Bruce was afraid that Gramps was putting his bag in the trunk of the wrong car, and then he saw that Gramps' shiny maroon sedan was wearing a mask of gray dust. Gramps didn't say a word as he drove to the airport exit that led to the San Diego Thruway. He clutched the steering wheel and leaned forward as if he'd never driven before. Cars whizzed by. Gramps poked along the Thruway at thirty-five miles an hour.

"Hate this Thruway," he muttered. "Damn fools think it's a racetrack. Jane was my navigator. Nothing is the same since she died." He banged the steering wheel with the palm of his hand.

Bruce had expected Gramps to be sad. He was supposed to be sad. Bruce hadn't expected him to be a different person.

Bruce thought about other summers. When he was seven and his sister was eleven, they had flown alone together to spend two weeks with Gram and Gramps. Every year after that he had gone for longer periods of time. This year Joyce was baby-sitting for a family at a lake in the mountains, but Bruce was planning to spend the whole summer in California.

Mom had warned him that it wouldn't be the same without Gram. "Gramps says he's getting along just fine, but I wonder if he's eating properly."

"He doesn't like to eat alone. We'll eat together and we'll do all the things we've always done together. He'll feel better if I'm there." Bruce knew that was true. He and Gramps had always had this special thing between them. They liked sports and chess; most of all they liked each other.

As they rode along in silence, Bruce thought about

how Gramps had been. *I'll make him feel better*, Bruce said to himself.

"Hey, Gramps, I bought a great book about swimming." Bruce tried to sound cheerful. "I want to swim every day and get to be really good this summer. You don't particularly like to swim, do you?"

Gramps didn't answer.

"We'll play tennis every day. And golf. Think the Old Duffers will let me drive the golf cart this year?"

Gramps didn't answer.

It was almost dark when they turned off the Thruway onto a busy street outside the Villa Verde walls. That was where Gramps lived, in a retirement village with five swimming pools, dozens of tennis courts and eighteen holes of golf. There was only one thing Villa Verde didn't have—kids.

The man at the gate of the village shouted a greeting, but Gramps didn't answer. He just drove on down the winding streets and parked the car in his carport.

He took the suitcases out of the trunk and walked ahead on the sidewalk and up the few steps to a porch, which was an entryway for his apartment and one other. He pushed open the door.

"You didn't lock your door?" Gram had been careful about locking the door, even though the village was surrounded by high walls and guarded gates.

"Nothing of value here—anymore." Gramps dropped the bags beside the door, ambled off to the living room, turned on the television and dropped into the big chair in front of it. Bruce followed him. Black pipe tobacco smudged the carpet in a circle around the chair. Brown leaves littered the windowsills and dusty tables around pots of brown stems. Gram's houseplants were all dead.

Gramps didn't offer him anything to eat or drink, but Bruce decided to help himself. He wasn't especially hungry, but he felt squirmy in a room with this man who was acting like a stranger. He took a carton of milk out of the refrigerator, sniffed it and emptied it down the drain.

Last summer there had been a huge chocolate cake on the counter. The refrigerator had been crowded with three kinds of juice, a couple of different soft drinks, a gallon of milk. Gramps could have bought a cake and a quart of fresh milk. Was that too much to expect?

Bruce drank a glass of water and went to the den, where he slept when he visited. The sofa bed had not been made up, so he found the blue-striped sheets for it in the linen closet. Gramps didn't come to help.

Last year he'd hardly had a chance to go to the bathroom because Gramps and Gram had been taking turns hugging him and telling him about all of the wonderful things they had planned. He couldn't expect it to be the same without Gram, but still. . . . His milk-shake summer was beginning to taste like turnips. If he'd been younger, he might have cried.

The phone rang but Gramps didn't answer it, so Bruce picked it up.

"We're in New York," Mom sang out. "We flew in

5

over Manhattan, and I could see Central Park and the Empire State Building. Dad says maybe we can spend a few days here on our way home. How was your flight? How's Gramps?"

"Flight was fine. Gramps was there."

"And?"

"It's not the same without Gram." Bruce gulped more air into his lungs. "There's not much to eat around here."

"That's just as I suspected. Gramps is probably living on pizza and French fries. He's got to eat properly."

Mom was a nut about wholesome food. If Bruce yelled at his sister, it wasn't because Joyce was a bratty teenager, it was because *he'd* had too much sugar. If he did poorly in school, it wasn't because he didn't pay attention but because he hadn't had enough protein in his breakfast.

"Now, Bruce, what I want you to do is this. See that Gramps has a good breakfast. . . ."

"Yes, Mom." Bruce decided not to tell her that there was nothing to make breakfast out of. "Is Gramps poor since Gram died? Maybe he can't afford . . ."

"Nonsense. Gramps is not rich, but he's not poor. Ask him to take you to the supermarket tomorrow. Buy what you'll need for your special roast-chicken dinner. Gramps will like that. And be sure you buy cheese and whole-grain breads, and granola for breakfast. And both of you take those vitamins I bought for you—every day."

Bruce sighed. Mom didn't understand how it was with Gramps. It was going to take more than a chicken and a pill.

"Are you sure you're going to be all right, dear? I don't have to go on this trip with Daddy. I could change my ticket and fly to California. . . ."

"No, Mom. Gramps and I are going to be just fine. We've already talked about playing golf with the Old Duffers. Maybe they'll let me drive the cart this year." It was just a *little* lie, and it would make Mom happy. She was looking forward to her summer vacation just as much as Bruce had been looking forward to his. "Good-bye, Mom. Have a good time."

"Wait, Bruce. You have our schedule. Call us anytime. You will do that, won't you, dear?"

"Sure, Mom. Good-bye."

Bruce sat on the end of the bed and thought. He had learned a lot about how to live with sadness during the past few months. First Gram had died. Then Goldie'd had to be put to sleep. She had been his for as long as he could remember. She was the best dog in the whole world.

He had spent the first two days after she was gone doing nothing. He couldn't swallow food. He had wanted to stay home from school, but his parents had made him go. His dad drove him—to make sure he got there. That was almost three months ago. He still missed Goldie—he'd always miss her—but not all the time.

Food wouldn't help Gramps much; doing things

would. Tomorrow they'd shop and play tennis and go to the pool. Gramps could sit in the sun, if he didn't want to swim. After dinner they'd watch a game or play chess. Later in the week they'd go to a game or to Disneyland. Gramps needed to do fun things. Then he'd feel better.

❧ 2 ❧

*B*ruce went to bed early by California time and woke up early. Gramps was sleeping in his chair; he hadn't gone to bed at all.

In the kitchen Bruce looked for something, anything, to eat. He found a line of busy ants on the kitchen counter.

Last night he'd thrown out the sour milk, but the refrigerator still smelled so awful that he wanted to gag. Mucky black blobs that might once have been lettuce clung to one shelf. He washed them away. At the back of another shelf he found a jar with white cotton growing out of it. He threw that away. Then a limp carrot. When the refrigerator was empty except for jars of mustard and salad dressing, he wiped it out with a wet paper towel.

In the freezer he found half a loaf of white bread. There was a jar of peanut butter in the cupboard, and a jar of instant coffee. He made himself a toasted peanut-butter sandwich and washed it, and a vitamin pill, down with water.

He had just finished eating when Gramps coughed behind him. "Morning, Gramps."

"Bruce? What are you doing here?"

"I came last night. Remember? You picked me up at the airport."

Gramps nodded and turned away.

"I'll have coffee and toast for you as soon as you get out of the shower." Bruce turned the heat on under the tea kettle.

When Gramps came back to the kitchen, Bruce set a peanut-butter sandwich and a mug of coffee in front of him. Gramps looked surprised, but he didn't say anything until Bruce had poured him a second mug of coffee.

"I meant to call your mother and tell her not to send you. This is no place for you. Call the airport and see when you can get a plane home." Gramps took his mug back to his chair in front of the television.

Bruce followed him and handed him a vitamin and a glass of water. "When Mom called, you said you wanted me to come."

Gramps shrugged his shoulders. "If I'd told her how things are with me, she'd have been on the next plane. She'd have made me do things I don't want to do."

"Sorry, Gramps, but I can't go home now. Mom and Dad are in London. Remember?"

Gramps nodded and switched on the set.

"Mom says we should take vitamins."

He didn't look up, but he took the pill.

"I think we should go shopping, don't you?" Bruce tried to sound cheerful.

Gramps didn't respond, so Bruce reached for the overflowing ashtray that was on the table beside his elbow. Gramps didn't look up then, or while Bruce was rounding up all the other ashtrays and dirty mugs and glasses and taking them to the dishwasher.

Bruce opened the door to the balcony to get rid of the old-smoke smell. He didn't want to do housework. He didn't want to be ignored. His shoulders felt stiff; his chest felt too full.

"What should we do with the dead plants?" he asked.

Gramps didn't answer, so he picked up a pot and put it in Gramps' lap. And then another. And another. Still Gramps ignored him. Bruce clenched his fists.

And then he exploded. "Why don't you get out of that chair and show me where to put these pots!" he shouted.

Gramps stared at him for a minute, and then he got to his feet and walked toward the door, carrying his three pots. Bruce followed with the rest of them. They dropped them into a trash bin outside.

"You going to vacuum up the rug?" Bruce asked as Gramps headed back to his chair.

Gramps shook his head and sat down.

Bruce stepped between Gramps and the television.

11

"Let's go shopping. Get us something to eat. A big juicy steak. Hamburger. Blueberry pie." Blueberry pie was Gramps' favorite.

Gramps looked at Bruce, but it wasn't a warm, friendly look; it was an angry glare. Then he nodded and shook his head and went to his room.

He returned to the living room with a laundry basket heaped with envelopes, which he put on the dining table.

"Just pull out anything that looks like a check or a bill. I'm afraid I've been neglecting my duties some." He grinned sheepishly.

Neglecting his duties! He hadn't even opened the card Bruce had sent him for Father's Day. Bruce opened a bill that said that unless Gramps paid for March, April and May, his electricity would be turned off. Gramps *was* poor, Bruce thought as he opened another envelope. It contained a check. Maybe he wasn't poor, but he was in a mess, a real mess.

"Think we should phone Mom and ask her what to do?"

Gramps banged his fist against the table and glared. "I can manage my own affairs, thank you. You may have forgotten that I am a certified public accountant. What do you think I did all my life? I managed other people's money."

Then manage your own, Bruce wanted to say.

He pulled out all the advertisements first and threw them in the wastebasket. Then he stacked the magazines. He put the handwritten letters and cards to one side. Many of them were from people telling Gramps how sorry they were Gram had died.

Everything else he put right under Gramps' nose, the checks in one pile, the bills in another. Whenever Gramps looked toward the television, Bruce slapped the pile of bills and waited until Gramps had written another check.

"I don't know how I could have been so careless," Gramps said when the basket was finally empty. "Guess we'd better deposit these checks right away—and mail off these payments."

"And buy food. Let's have lunch out."

It was mid afternoon when they got home. Gramps helped carry in the bags of groceries and put the stuff away. And then he sighed deeply and went to sit in front of the television.

Bruce took the large roasting chicken out of the plastic and pulled the package with the neck and the liver out of the bird. He ran water through the bird and dried it with paper towels, and then he rubbed a little butter in the bottom of a baking pan. He set the bird in the pan and rubbed butter onto the top of the bird all around the little thermometer that would pop up when the bird was done.

While the chicken was baking, he put the neck and the liver in a pan and covered them with water and let them simmer. He washed and sliced all the vegetables for a salad.

Then he didn't have anything to do for a while.

Gramps was sleeping in his chair while a dumb game show danced on the screen. Bruce went to his room and studied the book called *How to Swim and Dive Like a Champion*. He also read the first chapter of a science-fiction book he had brought with him. He checked on his chicken every half hour.

When the thermometer thing popped out and the chicken was done, Bruce took it out of the oven and put it on a platter. For the first time in his whole life, Bruce made gravy that wasn't lumpy. The stuffing was the instant kind that comes in a box. He poured dressing over the salad and opened a can of cranberry sauce.

Then he called Gramps to the kitchen. "There you have it," he sang out. "The Bruce Hardy non-Thanksgiving dinner. Mom said you'd carve the chicken."

Gramps didn't say anything, but he looked less glum as he carved. He didn't say anything during the meal, but he ate a lot. So did Bruce.

When they had each finished a big bowl of chocolate ice cream, Gramps rose, dropped his paper napkin in his plate and said, "Thanks, Bruce, that was the first good supper I've had since . . ." He turned and went back to his chair, leaving Bruce alone in the messy kitchen.

Back home the cook left the dining room as soon as the meal was over. Other members of the family cleaned up. Bruce began to feel himself getting angry again. He wasn't Gramps' slave.

But he set to work. The day hadn't been all bad. There was food in the refrigerator. Gramps had paid his bills. He'd said thanks for dinner. Maybe tomorrow Gramps would either cook or clean up, one or the other.

When the kitchen was clean, Bruce took the chess set from the bookshelf. He put the board on the table beside Gramps and began setting up the men. "I haven't played since you visited us at Christmas," he said.

Gramps stared at the board. Then he glared at Bruce. "And you're not going to play now. At least not with me." He swept his arm across the board, scattering the men across the carpet.

That did it! Bruce ran to the den and threw himself onto the bed. *He's your father*, he said to Mom, who wasn't there. *You can just get back on a plane and come take care of him yourself.*

Bruce knew he wasn't being fair; he'd begged Mom to let him come spend the summer with Gramps. Last night, while she was still in the United States, she would have come if Bruce had told her the truth about Gramps.

The door opened. "Just leave me to my grief, Bruce." Gramps did not enter the room. "You can't go home, because your parents are gallivanting in Europe. Jane is dead, and her only daughter is off gallivanting in Europe." He shook his head and turned back to the living room.

Bruce turned on the small television in the den, but he thought about what Gramps had said. Gramps was right. Mom should be at home feeling sad.

Then he remembered that Mom had been very sad

when she came home from Gram's funeral. For a few days she hadn't wanted to do anything or talk to anyone.

One night at dinner she sort of shook herself all over and said, "Life is for the living. We loved Gram. She was a good mother and a good grandmother, and we are lucky because we have so many happy memories."

They all talked about Gram then. They talked about her often. Then Dad announced that he had to go to Europe on business, and why didn't Mom come along? Joyce had been asked to baby-sit for the summer and Bruce had said he wanted to visit Gramps, so Mom had begun to read travel books.

It wasn't his mom's fault Bruce was stuck in California with someone who didn't want him. It wasn't his dad's fault either. It was partly his own fault; he'd wanted to come. Mostly it was the fault of that mean, lazy, gloomy old man who used to be his Good Buddy.

❧3❧

Gramps slept in his chair again that night, but he got up and made his own coffee.

Mom had felt better as soon as they had all started talking about Gram. Bruce liked to talk about Goldie. Maybe talking would help Gramps. While they were eating breakfast, Bruce tried to think of something natural to say about Gram.

He couldn't, so he asked about the Old Duffers. Last year Gramps hadn't allowed anything to interfere with his golf games with the Old Duffers. "Where are our clubs?" Bruce asked.

Gramps got up and returned to the kitchen with the clubs he had bought the previous summer for Bruce.

Bruce took a sock off one of the clubs. "Gram knit these for me. Must have taken her a long time. And she knit socks for your clubs too. Where are they?"

"I don't need my clubs. You go play without me. The Old Duffers will be glad to see you."

"No."

Bruce wasn't going to go off with strangers to walk around after a little ball. He played golf to be with Gramps, not because he thought it was such a fun game. "I'll go if you go. So come on." Bruce was pleading.

Gramps was not responding. He leaned the bag of clubs against the wall and started back to his chair. "Suit yourself," he muttered.

"Gram liked to have you play golf. She said it was good exercise."

"I wasted a lot of time playing golf when I could have been with her. Besides, every time I go out, I have to come home. I forget Jane won't be here. When I walk into this silent apartment and she's not here, I feel . . ." He turned on the set and lit his pipe.

Bruce brought Gramps his vitamin and a glass of orange juice. Then he drew up a chair and sat with him for a while—until they were watching an episode of *Lucy* Bruce had seen many times.

"I'd like to go swimming," Bruce announced.

"So go."

"Which pool? What hours?"

Certain of the Villa Verde pools were open to kids during certain hours. Gram had always kept track of when and where. Gramps got up and came back with a schedule. Bruce couldn't swim until after lunch. So what was he going to do all morning?

He went for a run, missing Goldie. She'd liked to run, until she started to get sick. He knew what Gramps meant about going out and expecting Gram to be there when he got back. Every time Bruce ran up the drive-way toward his house, there was this weird moment when he expected to hear Goldie bark.

His folks thought he should get another dog. They didn't expect Mom to adopt a new mom or Gramps to marry a new wife, but they wanted Bruce to get a new dog! There would never be a dog like Goldie.

He slowed down, like a toy that needs winding. He had lost Gram and Goldie—and now his Good Buddy. His parents were thousands of miles away. His friends were in Colorado. Even Joyce—*old lamb brain*—was too far away to fight with.

At that moment he would have been glad to hear her shout *Giraffe neck!* Sometimes he called her cow fat. That really made her mad. Bruce began to feel better and to run again.

All of the buildings in Villa Verde had red-tile roofs and adobe-colored walls. But they came in different styles. There were one-story buildings, and taller ones with elevators, and two-story buildings like Gramps' where you went down a few steps to a little courtyard and two apartments or up a few steps to a little porch and two more apartments. Everywhere there were flowers and lawns and palm trees. Bruce saw some silly little dogs and their owners carrying pooper scoopers.

And then he saw the Alien. She was walking away from one of the entrances, heading toward the wash-house, carrying a full laundry basket. When she saw Bruce, she stopped and stared. They were both Aliens in this village of old people. The girl Alien was also about twelve. She was short and round with straight hair pulled back in a ponytail. They were both wearing the Alien uniform, cut-off jeans and striped T-shirts.

She turned back toward the washhouse, but as she turned, she lifted three fingers from the basket and waved. Bruce waved too, and then laughed. Their waves were like an Alien handshake.

When Bruce got home he made sandwiches, and when they had eaten he asked Gramps to drive him to the pool. Gramps could have stayed to swim or sit in the sun and watch, but he didn't want to do either; he said he'd come back for Bruce at four o'clock.

At the pool, that very first day, he met Mac. Bruce had jumped in the deep end and was heading toward the shallow end, wishing he had checked the chapter in his book on the crawl. He kicked as hard and as fast as he could, but he was hardly moving. This old man jumped in behind him, swam around him to the shallow end and came back toward him. It was embarrassing to see an old man who could swim twice as fast as a kid.

They both kept on swimming for a while, the old man doing two laps to every one of Bruce's. He didn't even seem to be getting tired. Then he climbed out at the shallow end and motioned to Bruce, who *was* tired.

"Mind if I give you a few pointers?" Standing at the edge of the pool, he looked like the troll in "The Three Billy Goats Gruff." He was just a little taller than Bruce.

His muscles were like ropes clinging to his scrawny arms and legs.

"I don't look like much of a coach, but the brain still works. Coached some championship high-school teams. You could be a champion. Right build—and spirit." The old man laughed. "But you're working too hard."

"I want to be a fast swimmer. . . ."

"Then don't kick so hard. Here, hold on to the edge and kick like this—slow and loose, like your knees and your ankles were made of rubber bands." The Troll jumped in to demonstrate. Later he helped Bruce with arm strokes. And then they swam laps, side by side.

At the end of the afternoon they climbed out of the pool. The little man extended his hand. "Name is James MacGurdy. You can call me Mac or Coach. And you?"

"Bruce Hardy. I'm visiting my grandfather."

"I come to the pool every afternoon. Hope I'll see you again, Bruce. You've made amazing progress today. You could be a fine swimmer. Have a team in your school?"

Bruce couldn't believe it. It sounded like Mac was offering to coach him. "We don't have a pool at my school, but there's one in the high school. I'd like to . . . But I don't want to be a bother to you. . . ."

Mac slapped Bruce on the shoulder. "Bother me? I've spent my whole life with young people. I miss them. So let's get this straight, right off the bat. Anytime you swim with me, you'll be doing me a favor." He paused. "Your grandfather won't mind?"

21

Bruce didn't tell him that Gramps didn't give two hoots what he did so long as Bruce stayed out of his way.

The clock on the wall in the bathhouse said five o'clock. Five o'clock! Bruce threw on his clothes and ran to the parking lot. Gramps wasn't there. Why hadn't he waited, or come to the side of the pool to get him? Bruce walked home.

Gramps looked up from the television set when he came into the living room. "Bruce!" he said, as if surprised. Gramps had forgotten him again.

Bruce was only a little angry; he'd had such a good afternoon. "I've been swimming. Met a man who used to coach high-school teams. Gave me some pointers. Nice man. Maybe you know him. James MacGurdy."

Gramps shook his head and turned back to the news on television. Bruce stretched out on the couch and closed his eyes. He dreamed that Gram was puttering around in the kitchen.

"Sit up and eat." Gramps was shaking his shoulder. On the coffee table was a plate of thick sandwiches stuffed with chicken and lettuce and tomatoes. Gramps had brought out a carton of milk and a glass and a box of cookies. The Angels game had already begun, and they watched while they ate.

When the game was over, Gramps got up from his chair, locked the door and went to the bedroom. Bruce went to the den, but he had taken such a long nap that he wasn't sleepy. He finished the science-fiction book.

He was finally beginning to yawn when he heard

22

Gramps mumble. "Jane?" Then he shouted. "Jane! Where are you, Jane?"

Bruce's skin turned cold and creepy. Listening to his grandfather call to Gram was more frightening than any monster movie he could imagine. He kept thinking he should *do* something, but what? He clutched the sheet around his shoulders and shivered.

When Gramps went right on calling, Bruce got out of bed. He opened the door to Gramps' room. With the hall light on he could see him sitting up, staring at the wall beyond the foot of the bed.

Bruce crept toward him and touched his shoulder. "Gramps," he whispered. "Wake up, Gramps."

"Jane," he sighed, and reached out. Then he blinked. "You're not Jane." He pointed his finger at Bruce.

"I'm Bruce, your Good Buddy. You were having a bad dream."

"Jane was here. You call that a bad dream? You're a know-nothing like all the rest. Get out. Hear me, get out!" He swung his legs over the side of the bed, stood and pushed Bruce aside.

Back in his own bed Bruce sat hugging his knees to his chest and shivering. He was angry with Gramps for telling him to get out; Gramps should have known that Bruce was trying to help.

More than angry, Bruce was sad, because Gramps was so sad. Poor Gramps! Would Dad be like that if Mom died? Would Dad understand if Bruce called him and told him what was going on with Gramps? Could anyone understand unless they'd heard Gramps calling for Gram? Dad wouldn't let Bruce stay here if he knew, that was for sure. And then Gramps would be all alone again. Poor Gramps. Bruce could think of only one thing to do: He would stick by his Good Buddy just as long as he could.

The sky was turning gray when he finally fell asleep.

❧ 4 ❧

It was almost noon when Bruce woke, but Gramps was still in bed. He was just lying there, staring at the ceiling.

"Hi, Gramps," Bruce said. "It's too late for breakfast. How about lunch?"

Gramps didn't answer. He didn't even blink. Bruce crept out of the room. For a long time he leaned against the kitchen sink, trying to think what he should do.

If Gramps was sick, Bruce should call the doctor. He wasn't sick; he was sad, so sad that he couldn't think about anyone but himself. He could—he should—have been doing things around the house, playing golf with the Old Duffers, playing tennis with Bruce and driving him to his swimming lessons. Instead he was lying in bed, feeling sorry for himself.

Bruce felt sorry for himself too. He'd expected to be doing fun things with his Good Buddy, not playing housekeeper to a glum old man. He had no friends his own age. He had no friends of any age in the whole state of California—except Mac.

He was mad; he was sad; he was hungry. While he was making a sandwich for himself, he remembered the sandwich Gramps had made for him the night before—they'd had a good time watching the game together. Bruce made a second sandwich and a cup of coffee. He left the sandwich on the counter with a napkin over it. He took the coffee to Gramps' room.

"Drink this coffee, Gramps," he begged. "I've left a sandwich for you on the kitchen counter."

Gramps didn't move.

"If you're sick, I'll call the doctor. Are you sick?"

Gramps didn't answer.

"I'm a kid, in case you've forgotten. Mom wants me to see that you eat properly. I can't make you eat, and it isn't my fault you're unhappy. So I'm going to go swimming now. Mac will be glad to see me, even if you're not."

Bruce waited for Gramps to say something, and then he ran to the front door. He let the door slam behind him. He ran until he got a stitch in his side.

Mac called a greeting. He got out of the pool and peered into Bruce's face. "You okay, Bruce?"

Tears rose behind his eyes, and he jumped into the pool and began to swim. Mac swam beside him, back and forth and back and forth, the crawl and then the backstroke. When they stopped to rest, Mac peered at him again and asked if he wanted to learn the racing dive. By the end of the afternoon, he could dive far out into the pool.

"Never saw an athlete learn so fast," Mac said as they headed for the dressing room.

The coach called Bruce an athlete! He grinned up into Mac's eyes.

"You feeling better?" Mac asked.

Bruce continued to grin and nodded. He did feel better.

Mac said that he and his wife were going to San Diego for the weekend. He'd be back Monday. "Maybe you'd like to start diving from the board."

The sandwich was still sitting on the counter. Bruce forced himself down the hall to Gramps' room. There was scum on top of the coffee. And then he looked at Gramps. He was still staring at the ceiling. Had he moved all afternoon?

"Please get up, Gramps. I'll cook you a terrific dinner. I'll . . . I'll do anything you want me to do. Please, Gramps."

Suddenly Gramps turned over and propped his head up on his hand. He looked straight at Bruce and glared. "Just leave me alone. Is that too much to ask?" He flopped back on the mattress and closed his eyes.

Once again Bruce left the apartment. He didn't notice where he was going, he didn't care, he just had to get out of there. And then he saw that he was on the street where he had seen the Alien.

There she was, running toward him with a big black dog whose ears flapped like wings and whose tail waved like a flag. When Bruce said, "Hi, dog," and reached out to pat him, the dog jumped up with his paws on Bruce's chest and began to lick his chin. He stroked him from the top of his head right down his flanks, the way Goldie had liked to be stroked. "What's your name?"

"My name is Othello Canine." The girl spoke in a voice that was between a bark and a growl. "What's a kid like you doing here with the old folks?"

"What do you mean?" He made his voice quaver, and bent his body as if he were leaning on a cane. "I'm eighty-seven years old. You?"

"Dog-sitting . . . dog-running." The girl spoke in a normal, friendly voice. "My great aunt had to have an operation. We kept the dog for her while she was in the hospital, and now I'm staying with her for the summer to take care of Ottie and see that Auntie doesn't overdo. And you?"

"I just told you. I'm eighty-seven. I own an apartment here." Bruce laughed, which felt good. "I'm visiting my grandfather. My name's Bruce Hardy, like in the Hardy boys."

"I'm Jenny Duncan, not Nancy Drew."

Jenny handed him the leash, and the three of them walked along together.

"I had a dog named Goldie. . . ."

"A golden retriever?"

Bruce nodded and then said something he hadn't thought he'd ever say to a stranger. "Goldie had to be put to sleep in March. She couldn't walk anymore, and she was deaf. I should have let my dad take her to the vet sooner, but I couldn't. I just couldn't."

"I have a mutt named Schnoodle. . . ."

"Schnauzer and poodle?"

"Right. Before her I had a mostly Irish setter. He got hit by a car. He had to be put to sleep too. I know how you feel about Goldie."

She didn't give Bruce the lecture about how kind it is to have your dog killed. He appreciated that.

Ottie was pulling at the leash, begging for a run. Bruce ran with him, as fast as he could. He wished he could let go of the leash so that Ottie could run even faster, but there was a law in Villa Verde that every dog, no matter how old or how small, had to be leashed.

When they turned back onto Jenny's street, Ottie pulled him toward a stoop. A little old lady was bent over her walker, but she looked up and smiled first at Ottie and then at Bruce and Jenny.

"You are one lucky dog," she said as she scratched Ottie's head, "to have two children to give you the kinds of runs you love." She turned to Bruce. "I'll tell you a secret if you promise not to tell." She didn't wait for him to promise. "Sometimes, late at night when there is no one around, I let Ottie off the leash so he can give himself a run. He needs the exercise. Other times I walk just as fast as I can with him. Why don't

29

you young people go over to the clubhouse and play Ping-Pong? It will be a treat for Jenny to have someone besides an old lady to talk with."

"My mom says you are the youngest old lady in the whole world," Jenny said as she kissed the old lady's cheek.

The room was empty except for two men shooting pool. Bruce was not very good at Ping-Pong and Jenny was worse, so they just whacked the ball back and forth. They didn't even bother to keep score.

He felt better when he walked back to Gramps' apartment. Ottie and Jenny had done that. Ottie was a lot like Goldie—not as pretty, but kindhearted. He could tell Goldie his troubles, and she'd look at him as if she understood every word and was one hundred percent on his side—even when he knew he'd been wrong. Ottie had that kind of face.

The sandwich had disappeared from the kitchen counter. The door to Gramps' room was closed. Gramps had been up; that was a good sign. Bruce hoped he was now in bed *sleeping*. He heated a can of soup for himself.

❧5❧

When Bruce went to the kitchen the next morning, Gramps was there, his elbows on the counter, his head in his hands. He lifted his head and took a sip of coffee from the mug in front of him, and then he cleared his throat. "I'm sorry about yesterday, Bruce," he said. "Did you enjoy your swim?"

"Mac's coaching me. He taught me the racing dive."

"Good. You'll have another lesson today?"

"Mac and his wife have gone to San Diego. I'll just swim laps." He buttered his toast and sat down beside Gramps at the counter.

"I've been neglecting you," Gramps said at last. "Jane wouldn't have liked that. She wanted us to be superior grandparents to you and Joyce. That was important to her."

"You were."

"It's just so hard for me to do anything these days. Anything at all."

31

"We did lots of fun things last year, didn't we?"

Gramps nodded. "Jane planned it all." He poured himself another mug of coffee. "There are some good games on television this afternoon. Anything you want to do . . ."

"We could play some tennis." Bruce crossed his fingers, hoping. *Let Gramps want to play tennis.*

"I'm out of shape." Gramps got up and headed for the TV, and then he shook himself. "How about the driving range?"

Bruce hadn't swung a golf club since last summer, and Gramps hadn't swung one since before Gram had died. They were both rusty, but they had fun.

They stopped for hamburgers at a fast-food place, and then they went to the supermarket. Bruce found a blueberry pie in the freezer section. When they got home, the first game was just beginning.

Bruce skipped part of the second game to swim for an hour. He tried to remember everything Mac had told him.

As he was walking home from the pool, he realized that he was having the kind of smooth, sweet day he had imagined. At last!

Mr. and Mrs. Byrd, Gramps' neighbors, came out of their apartment as he was climbing the few stairs to the little porch outside Gramps' door. Last year Bruce had decided that Mrs. Byrd looked like a scrawny chicken, with her little beaklike nose. Mr. Byrd looked like a penguin; he had a big body and short legs.

"We didn't know you were here, Bruce, until I

saw you and your grandfather go out with your clubs this morning. That's good, very good," Mrs. Byrd clucked.

"Your grandfather's quit playing golf with us Old Duffers, you know, but he's always welcome. So are you." Mr. Byrd slapped Bruce on the back. "You can drive my golf cart, if you like."

"I don't think your grandfather has been eating properly," said Mrs. Byrd. "I took some food to him, but he never ate it. I invited him to eat with us, but he never showed up. But now you're here. I've fixed you this nice tuna casserole."

She handed a dish to Bruce and gave him detailed instructions about how long it was to be baked. *No wonder Gramps hadn't been eating the dishes Mrs. Byrd prepared for him. He hated tuna fish*, Bruce thought as he put the casserole in the refrigerator.

During the commercials he fried hamburger and added a jar of tomato sauce. He cooked spaghetti and made a big salad and heated the pie in the oven. They ate in front of the television set.

"Tastes like blue paste," Gramps said of the pie, but he grinned and ate it. And then *Gramps* cleared away the food and loaded the dishwasher.

When Bruce had visited before, they had always gone to church. This first Sunday of this visit, he went to the kitchen in his pajamas to ask Gramps if he should wear his Sunday slacks.

"Hymns make me cry. I thought we'd have brunch

33

at the hotel down by the beach before the games begin. Okay?" He rubbed his hand across his hairy jaw.

"You growing a beard, Gramps?"

"Jane hated beards. She wouldn't let me grow one. What do you think, Bruce?"

"I think beards are neat."

Gramps trimmed his beard, and then he brought out a mountain of laundry and put the dark stuff in one basket and the light stuff in another. Bruce added his dirty clothes. Gramps said they'd wash while they were watching the games.

Gramps drove to a hotel with a dining room overlooking the ocean. It was a buffet brunch, and Gramps kept sending Bruce back for more food. He asked questions about the swimming lessons and about his folks' trip and about the lake where Joyce was baby-sitting.

As they were leaving, he clapped Bruce on the shoulder. It was the first time he had done that since Bruce had arrived. "Good thing every customer isn't a growing boy, or this place would go out of business." He laughed. It was good to hear Gramps laugh.

They walked along the beach for a while. On the way back to the car they passed a bookstore, and Gramps insisted on buying Bruce some books. "I may go into a blue funk again, and you'll need something to read."

The phone was ringing when they entered the apartment—Dad phoning from Paris. "Is everything okay,

Bruce? Are you and Gramps having a good time together?"

"Sure, Dad. We had brunch down at the beach, and
now we're going to put our dirty clothes in the washing
machines and watch the game." Bruce decided not to
tell his dad how Gramps *had* been; everything was fine
now.

"I called Joyce and she's fine too, so now your
mother won't have a thing to worry about, except her
French. Actually she speaks it very well. You should
have heard her try to tell a lady with a cold that she
should take vitamin C. She said the whole thing in
French, and the lady understood." Dad laughed heart-
ily. "Mom said to give her love to the California bachelors. Mine too."

Bruce was still laughing when he hung up. He was
glad he hadn't told his parents about how Gramps had
been.

The California bachelors loaded all four of the machines in the washhouse before the game started. During one commercial they both ran out and transferred
everything from the washers to the dryers. During another commercial they brought the dry clothes into the
living room and folded them in front of the television.

When the game was over, Gramps offered to drive
Bruce to the pool, but Bruce said he liked the walk.

Jenny was sitting on the steps in front of her aunt's
apartment, reading a book. Bruce stopped to tell her
all of the things he and Gramps had done in the last
two days.

"That sounds great. Really great. I had the feeling that things weren't so good with you and your grandfather."

"They weren't." Bruce didn't want to say more about Gramps, so he asked a question. "How are things with you and your aunt? Do you have fun together?"

"I'm afraid Jenny has a very boring time here." They looked up to see Jenny's aunt standing behind the screen door. "The doctor won't let me go anyplace for another three weeks, so Jenny is stuck."

Jenny's face was bright red. "I don't feel stuck," she said.

"That's one of the things that make you so precious to me; you are so cheerful. I may never let you go home." Her aunt smiled at her, and then she opened the screen door and held a ten-dollar bill in front of Bruce. "You would be doing me a favor, young man, if you would take this girl away from here for an hour or so. Go to the gate and turn right. There's an ice-cream parlor in the next block. Have something big and gooey."

Jenny looked at Bruce. Her face was still red—or red again. "I think Bruce was going swimming. He . . ."

Bruce grinned. "My coach is away, so I don't have to swim today." He took the bill. "Thanks. What's your favorite kind of ice cream?" he asked Jenny.

At home Bruce's friends were all boys. He felt awkward walking down the sidewalk with Jenny at first, and then he reminded himself that she was the only kid he had seen all week. "You're not a girl," he said.

She looked at him and then turned her face away.

"You're an Alien. So am I. That's what I thought the first time I saw you. We're two Aliens in a whole planet of old folks."

"You like science fiction? Auntie had never seen *Star Trek* until I came. Can you believe that? I'm getting pretty tired of some of the reruns, but Auntie likes them. She says she's in love with Mr. Spock."

The Aliens ordered "zombies," made with three different kinds of ice cream, chocolate syrup, butterscotch syrup, marshmallow, whipped cream, nuts and a cherry. They decided that zombies would be the official Alien food.

As soon as he entered the living room, Bruce knew that the Blue Funk was back. Gramps looked up from the television just long enough to glare.

"Thought you'd forgotten about my dinner. Jane knew I liked to eat at six o'clock sharp."

"What happened while I was gone?"

"Women can't leave me alone. One of 'em came by just after you left. You should have been here to answer the door and tell her to go home. One of Jane's friends. She wanted me to play cards. My wife of forty-two years has just died, and the old biddy wanted me to play cards. She left a cake. What do I want with her damn cake? So where's my dinner?"

Bruce wanted to turn around and go right back out the door. Gramps *could* be nice like he used to be. He'd been nice for almost two days. So why didn't he just stay that way? Did Gramps *want* to make Bruce feel miserable?

Gramps didn't like tuna fish, but Bruce didn't care. It wasn't his fault the lady had come. He hadn't invited her. And he wasn't Gramps' servant. He put the tuna casserole in the oven.

Gramps ate it (it was pretty good) and the cake (it was delicious).

Bruce left the plates on the table—let Gramps clear up—and went to Jenny's. They ran Ottie and put him back inside, and then Bruce slumped down on the stoop and buried his head in his hands. He felt sad, and mad. Why couldn't Gramps have just said "Go away" to the lady with the chocolate cake—and to the Blue Funk?

"Want to tell me what happened?" Jenny asked. "You were happy this afternoon, and you are definitely not happy now."

"Wish Goldie were here. She'd understand."

"Pretend I'm Goldie." Jenny squatted down in front of Bruce and looked up into his face.

He told her about Gramps. "That guy I'm living with just isn't my grandfather. He's a yo-yo. Sometimes he doesn't seem to know I'm there. Then he notices me and gets mad. He treats me like a servant. 'Where's my dinner?' Why doesn't he do some of the cooking?"

Jenny stuck out her tongue and leaned forward as if to lick his arm. That's just what Goldie would have done, only Goldie would have actually licked; Jenny just pretended. She started to smile, but then she remembered she was a dog and gave a friendly yip.

"Gramps and I used to have so much fun together. Last summer we played tennis and golf, and at night when there wasn't a game on, we played chess. He took me to a couple of games and to Disneyland. The best times were when we just talked. He asked me what I thought about God, and he told me what he thought. He told me stories about his grandpa. He told me how important I was to him. This summer I don't matter at all. He can't think about anyone except himself and how sad he is because Gram died. I miss Gram too." He turned away.

Jenny patted his foot. Goldie used to do that. Bruce reached out and scratched Jenny's head. They both laughed.

When Bruce got home, the living room was empty, but the dinner plates had been cleared away and the counter wiped clean. The door to Gramps' room was closed.

❦ 6 ❦

The Blue Funk was sitting on Gramps' shoulder on Monday morning. He ate his breakfast in silence and then went to sit in front of the television.

Okay, Gramps, sit there and feel sorry for yourself. I don't care. Bruce got his racket and went to the tennis courts. *Take that, Blue Funk.* He slammed the ball against the backboard. *And that.*

Gramps didn't care about him, but Mac did. He grinned broadly when Bruce dove into the pool to swim along beside him that afternoon. They worked on dives from the board.

Back in the dressing room Mac suddenly turned to Bruce. "You a dog lover by any chance?" He didn't wait for an answer; maybe he saw it in Bruce's face. "Would you and your grandfather be able to keep a dog for a couple of weeks?"

40

He went on to explain that the widow who lived in the apartment above his had had a stroke in the night. She'd been taken to the hospital, which meant that her dog was alone. Mac had fed it and walked it that morning, but Mac's wife was allergic to dogs, so they couldn't invite the dog to stay in their apartment.

"The dog's name is Vanessa—of all things. She's a funny—very funny—looking mutt," Mac said. "She's been spoiled. Treated like a child. Her owner coos over her and cooks for her and lets her sleep in her bed at night."

"Is she housebroken?"

"Yes. And spayed."

Bruce rubbed his fingers down his cheeks and tried to think. "My grandmother died in March, and Gramps is sad and lonely. Sometimes he doesn't do anything all day long, just sits in his chair in front of the television. If he had a dog, he'd have to get up to walk it. . . ."

"Old people need exercise—and friends," said Mac. "Vanessa is young and friendly; she demands long walks, and she'd introduce him to other dog walkers."

"Gramps probably wouldn't like her. I don't think he's ever had a dog. My grandmother was afraid of dogs. How long would it be for?"

"Frankly, I doubt that Vanessa's owner will ever be able to live alone again, but if I knew that for sure, I'd just take the dog to the pound. Thing is, I don't know, and if she comes home and Vanessa isn't there . . . In the meantime, it would give your grandfather a chance to find out if a dog would suit him. If he found that he enjoyed Vanessa's company, he could go to the pound and pick his own dog. Male or female. Young or old. Large or small. . . ."

Bruce shook his head. He just didn't know. Last summer Gramps would have done almost anything to help an old lady in the hospital, whether he knew her or not. But this year . . .

"Why don't you talk it over with your grandfather? Here's my number; call me tonight."

Bruce talked it over with Jenny, instead. She agreed that a dog would be good for Gramps.

"You'll have to go home before school starts, and then . . . I'm not saying that a dog would take your place, but still, a dog is good company, and besides, a dog would be good company for you while you're here. We could walk the dogs together—if they like each other."

After dinner Bruce and Jenny went to Mac's apartment, where they met his wife, a tiny lady in a wheelchair.

"I'm so glad you're here, Bruce," she said. "My Mac gets up singing every morning now that he has another student. Once a teacher, always a teacher."

"So your grandfather's agreed to take the dog," Mac boomed. "Surprised he didn't come with you. But we'd rather see this pretty little girl than another old person. Let's go meet Vanessa."

"This is just a trial," Bruce whispered. "Gramps may

42

not take to her." He wasn't telling Mac the whole truth about Gramps, and that made him uncomfortable.

"Understood. You can bring her back tomorrow if you want, though I'm afraid I'd have to take her to the pound...." That wasn't fair. It was hard enough to put Goldie to sleep, but to kill a young dog... That's what they do to dogs that don't get adopted right away.

Vanessa would never be adopted. Bruce knew that as soon as he saw her. Her wiry hair—gray, tan and white—stood out all over her body so that she looked a little like a porcupine. Her legs were too long for her body. Her face had a few whiskers, she had a topknot held back in a red barrette. How could anyone take to this dog?

All he could say for her was that she was friendly. She jumped up on Bruce and then she jumped on Jenny, her whole body wiggling with joy.

"Okay, Vanessa, time to go." Mac snapped a leash on her collar and put her pink dish and her brush and some cans of dog food in a shopping bag. "Well, mutt, this is it. I hope you can manage to endear yourself to Bruce's grandfather." Mac patted Vanessa, who wagged her tail and licked his hand as if promising to do her best.

"She sure is ugly," Bruce said to Jenny as soon as they were away from Mac's building. "Gramps wouldn't be able to resist a dog like Goldie or Ottie, but Vanessa?"

"Beauty is skin deep. Maybe Vanessa has a great personality." Jenny laughed. "At least she's friendly."

"Maybe she's a dog genius," Bruce suggested, though it didn't seem at all likely.

Vanessa walked along nicely until she spotted a squirrel, and then she strained at the leash and yelped and barked until people came to their doors to see what was going on.

"Kids," one of them muttered loudly. "We were assured when we moved here that we would not be bothered with children."

"The kids aren't disturbing the peace," Bruce whispered so only Jenny could hear. "It's this poorly trained senior citizen's dog that's making all the noise."

"Shut up, Vanessa." Jenny grabbed the dog's nose and held her mouth closed so that she could not bark.

The closer they got to Gramps' apartment, the slower Bruce walked. Jenny must have noticed, because she walked right past her aunt's and continued on with him.

They entered the living room with Vanessa still on the leash. Gramps looked away from his televison set. "What have we here? A lovely young lady and her dog. How do you do?" Gramps greeted Jenny and Vanessa very politely.

"It's not my dog," Jenny said after she had greeted Gramps.

"Oh?" Gramps' eyebrows shot up. "Is that Goldie?"

"Goldie's dead." Gramps knew that.

"Oh, yes. Your mother said you got rid of her. Said you were all upset about it. Is this your new Goldie? She's not as good-looking as the original, I must say."

Jenny gasped when Gramps said "you got rid of her." Jenny knew that he hadn't gotten rid of her like you get rid of a candy wrapper. She knew how much it hurt to put a dog you loved to sleep.

"There will never be another Goldie!" If Bruce hadn't shouted, he would have choked. "This is Vanessa. We're dog-sitting her. Mac's neighbor is in the hospital, and Mrs. Mac is allergic to dogs. Vanessa needs a home for a few weeks. Mac's been very good to me, and Vanessa will have to go to the pound to be put to sleep if . . . and she's a very young dog . . . and housebroken . . . and spayed . . . and . . ."

"Enough!" Gramps bellowed. "You know your grandmother is afraid of dogs."

"Gram *was* afraid of dogs." *And now she's dead too.* "I'll take care of Vanessa until her owner's well. You don't even have to look at her if you don't want to."

"Fine. I won't."

Bruce yanked at Vanessa's leash and pulled her out of the apartment. Jenny followed. She didn't say anything until they got to her door. "I'm sorry . . ." She hung her head. Then she touched his hand and scooted inside.

Bruce began training Vanessa the first night. She wanted to sleep on the bed with him; only Goldie could do that. Every time she climbed up, Bruce pushed her down. Finally she went to sleep beside the bed with Bruce's hand on her head.

The first sound he heard the next morning was a roar from Gramps' room. "What is this damn dog doing on my bed? Get out! Hear me? Get off this bed!"

Vanessa, tail between her legs, came back to the den and lay down on the rug. Bruce tried to explain to her that she would have to stay away from Gramps. She misunderstood and thought he was saying something nice. She stood up wagging her tail, and then she climbed onto his bed.

Bruce pushed her off and tried, once again, to warn her about Gramps. "He doesn't like you. Take my word, he'll use any excuse to get rid of you. So you've got to behave perfectly, absolutely perfectly, if you want to stay here until you can go back home."

Vanessa said that she understood, or at least she sat on her haunches and looked at him in a friendly sort of way. He dressed quickly, snapped on Vanessa's leash and took her outside.

"There are pooper scooper laws here," Gramps called. "I will not have the neighbors complaining that your dog is a nuisance."

Bruce went back to the kitchen and picked up a newspaper. Out on the road Vanessa squatted, and then she looked at Bruce and waited. She waited until he put the paper under her, and then she did her business. She *was* smart.

"Good dog." Bruce rewarded her by scratching her head. Then he gathered up the paper and took it to a trash bin, and they walked toward Jenny's. Jenny and Ottie were walking too. While the two dogs sniffed each other, he told Jenny about Vanessa's one sign of intelligence.

"Or training," Jenny said. "At least she can be trained."

Whenever he went out, Bruce locked Vanessa in the den. She spent most of her days in there, but she never complained. Her treat came after dinner, when Jenny and Bruce gave Ottie and Vanessa long runs.

Bruce's days depended on the yo-yo. When Gramps was in a good mood, they ate out and went to the driving range. Gramps cleaned up after dinners at home. One day he even got out the vacuum and cleaned all of the carpeting while Bruce dusted the furniture.

When Gramps was in a good mood, Bruce let Vanessa into the living room to lie beside him while they watched the game in the evening. Gramps never seemed to notice her, but at least he never complained about buying dog food.

When the Blue Funk was sitting on Gramps' shoulder, the days were not good. Gramps was silent or complaining. On those days Bruce felt like a donkey he had seen in a picture, burdened down with more than he could carry.

On one of those bad days Bruce tried to make Gramps feel better by cooking something different, pork chops.

"Tastes like shoe leather," Gramps grumbled. "Jane knew I liked potatoes. Why don't you fix potatoes for me?"

Because I don't want to peel potatoes. The next time they went shopping, Bruce asked the man in the vegetable department about baking potatoes, bought some and fixed them for Gramps. They didn't have to be peeled.

"Jane knew that I liked mashed potatoes." Gramps was like a whiny little kid.

Bruce gave up trying to please Gramps with food. The next time they went shopping, he filled the cart with TV dinners. They weren't good, but they were easy.

❀ 7 ❀

Vanessa had been living with Bruce for almost three weeks when Mac told him that her owner had died. "How's your grandfather getting along with the dog?"

"She's a good dog." Bruce sidestepped Mac's question.

"You don't want to get too attached to her. I'd hoped your grandfather would want to keep her, but if he doesn't, I'll take her to the pound. You know, Bruce, she's a young dog, and she has a very good chance of being adopted by someone who will give her a good home."

Bruce didn't believe that. No one would choose a dog as ugly as Vanessa.

He decided to tell Gramps about Vanessa's owner right away, get it over with. But when he got home from the pool, Vanessa was waiting at the outside door. Could he have left the den door unlatched? He didn't think so. He was always very careful about that. She couldn't have turned the knob herself.

Gramps wouldn't have let her out. He had been sitting in front of the television set with his Blue Funk for two days. He was no more aware of Vanessa than he was of Bruce. That's what Bruce thought until he entered the living room.

"I don't know why you shut up that dog all day every day." Gramps scowled. "Would you want to be locked up while your master was out gallivanting? The dog gets lonely. Did you ever think of that?" He turned back to the television, his pipe clenched in one hand. His other hand was resting on Vanessa's head.

Gramps was beginning to notice Vanessa! Maybe he was beginning to like her. It was too soon to tell. Bruce decided to wait a few days to tell Gramps about Vanessa's owner.

"It's up to you," he said to the dog when they were alone. "If you can make Gramps like you, you might have a home here. It's not the greatest place in the world, but it's better than the pound."

The next morning the Blue Funk was still there. *Why doesn't he just tell it to leave?* Bruce asked himself. *Because he likes to sit there and suffer. That's why.* Bruce was tired of Gramps' self-pity. *He needs exercise. If he wanted to feel better, he would leave the Blue Funk home with Vanessa and come hit tennis balls with me.*

"Let's go play tennis, Gramps. You're in better shape

now since we've been hitting balls at the driving range."

Gramps pretended he couldn't hear. Bruce went to the closet, hunted until he found Gramps' racket and a new can of balls and then took them into the living room. He switched off the set and stood with his back to it.

"Come on, Gramps. Please come play tennis with me. I wanted to become a good swimmer this summer, and Mac is helping me do it. But I also wanted to get better at tennis. I can't play by myself. . . ."

"Have you asked the sainted Mac?" Gramps snarled. "He does everything you like. He probably plays tennis."

"No!" Bruce shouted. "You're my grandfather and my tennis buddy. Get out of the chair and play with me." Bruce went to the bedroom and found Gramps' tennis sneakers. He knelt in front of Gramps and began to pull off his slippers.

Gramps kicked him—his grandfather actually kicked him! Then Gramps put his sneakers on and picked up his racket. Neither of them said anything as they marched to the courts.

Bruce was mad; Gramps had *kicked* him. He ran to the far side of the net and served a ball to Gramps, who just stood there, his hands at his side, and watched it bounce beside him. Bruce hit another, easier ball. Gramps raised his racket and shoved it into the net.

Bruce hit a third ball gently into Gramps' court. Gramps scooped it back over the net slowly. He wasn't even trying to make the game fun. He was just standing there showing Bruce how much he didn't want to play.

Bruce, madder than he had ever been before in his whole life, slammed the next ball straight at Gramps and ran toward the net. Gramps scowled and drove the ball back over Bruce's head. Bruce ran back and back and gave the ball a mighty blow. "Take that!" he shouted.

"Damn kid." Gramps smacked the ball so that it barely skimmed the net and came toward Bruce like a bullet aimed for his heart.

You've been trying to get rid of me ever since I got here. Now you're trying to kill me, Bruce thought as he whacked the ball with all his might.

It didn't seem possible that Gramps could hit the ball any harder, but he did. He was mad too. That was for sure.

Bruce whacked the ball back to Gramps. *I have a right to be angry. You've treated me like a servant— when you've noticed me at all.*

Whack!

And you said I got rid of Goldie. Thinking about what Gramps had said about Goldie gave Bruce added strength. He slammed the ball across the net. He whacked Gramps' return.

Bruce felt ready to explode. He ran from one side of the court to the other, from the net to the baseline, hitting the ball with every ounce of his strength.

Gramps did the same, scowling. Then Gramps hit a

ball that caught the top of the net and dropped over. Bruce ran forward and scooped it up and back toward Gramps, who gave it a blow to the back of the court. Bruce ran back again and reached it just in time.

"Great save!" Gramps shouted, and returned an easier ball. "Keep it up."

Bruce was tired, but he hit the ball as best he could. Gramps was grinning. Bruce grinned too. Back and forth the ball sailed, not gently, but no longer violently.

His racket felt like it was made of lead. His sides ached. His knees felt like jelly. Bruce dropped down in the middle of the court and rested his head on his knees.

Gramps was gasping for breath. He sounded like a locomotive. Bruce heard something else—clapping. When he turned his head, he saw a row of other tennis players standing on the sidelines. He wondered how long they had been watching them play. Play? It had been a war.

"That beard must be giving you strength, John," one of the spectators shouted. "Never saw so much energy on a Villa Verde court."

"It wasn't the beard," Gramps gasped. "It was the boy. Ever see a kid play like that? He's my grandson."

Bruce rose to his feet, and they staggered toward home, Gramps' arm around Bruce's shoulder.

Gramps went straight to his room. Bruce heard the shower and then nothing. When he went to check on Gramps, he was asleep. Bruce took a nap too, but he set the alarm so he wouldn't miss his swimming lesson.

He might just as well have skipped it; he didn't have the strength to do anything more than float.

"You don't seem to have much energy this afternoon," Mac commented.

"Sorry. Gramps and I played tennis this morning like . . ." He couldn't explain that tennis match. They'd both been so mad at one another at the beginning. At the end Gramps had said "my grandson" like he used to say it.

When Bruce got out of the pool, Gramps was standing there. "Thought the boy might need a ride home," he said to Mac. "You the coach? Want to thank you. Bruce says you've been a good friend to him. He's needed a friend."

Mac nodded. "He's not much good today. I guess you two had a real workout on the tennis courts this morning."

"He darn near killed me." Gramps chuckled.

"You're a lucky man," Mac said, "to be Bruce's grandfather."

"I know it. Believe me." Gramps clapped Bruce on the shoulder.

He didn't drive home; he drove to a restaurant and ordered steaks for both of them.

Gramps was in a good mood. Bruce should have told him then about Vanessa's owner.

After breakfast the next morning Gramps limped over to the television set, turned it on and lit his pipe. That's what he had done every morning, but this morning he had an excuse. He was stiff and had a blister on his heel.

Bruce was a little stiff too, so he went to his room to write to his folks. Vanessa lay on the floor beside him. From time to time he reached down to scratch her head. Then he reached down and there was nothing to scratch but air.

He found Vanessa in the living room, lying beside Gramps' chair. The television set was off, and Gramps was reading a magazine. He wasn't paying any attention to Vanessa.

Gramps reading instead of watching television was one surprise. And there was another. Gramps called Bruce to lunch. He had heated a can of chili himself!

That afternoon Bruce swam better than ever before, and he made a perfect low dive. Mac beamed and told him again that he could be a champion swimmer if he continued to progress as he had done that summer.

From that time on everything was better. Gramps' blister healed, and they began to play tennis most mornings. They never again played as well as they had played when they were mad at each other, but they had more fun.

"I don't like TV dinners," Gramps said once. "I don't suppose you do either. Too bad neither of us likes to cook." He began making salads to go with the dinners.

One Saturday they washed the car, and then they drove to San Diego. They went to the zoo and to a

Padres game. On the way home Bruce remembered the last time he had driven on the San Diego Thruway. This time Gramps was relaxed, and he drove at the speed limit. Gramps was well!

Jenny had walked Vanessa once while they were gone. Nevertheless the dog acted as if she had been abandoned. As they walked in the door, she barked excitedly and jumped up on Bruce. He hugged her. And then Vanessa jumped on Gramps. There was a moment—just an instant—when Bruce thought Gramps might pat her. Instead he pushed her down and went to his room.

When Mom phoned from Rome, Bruce told her the whole truth. Gramps was sometimes sad, but they were having a good time. They were eating well and taking their vitamins. And they were exercising. Twice a week they played golf with the Old Duffers; other days they played tennis.

Bruce did not tell Mac the truth about Vanessa.

"Whenever I ask you about that dog, you change the subject," Mac said to him one day. "Your grandfather doesn't want the dog? That's his right. Do you want me to come and get her, or will you bring her to my house?"

"Neither," Bruce almost shouted. "Please, Mac, give me a little more time. Gramps is much better. He's getting exercise and eating good food. . . ."

"Is he walking Vanessa?"

"No, but he will, just as soon as he notices her. He doesn't complain about her. She's really a nice dog.

I've trained her so that she stays off the bed. Gramps would like her if he knew her just a little better. Really he would."

Mac patted Bruce's shoulder. "All right, son, we'll give him a little longer to get to know that silly-looking mutt."

❧ 8 ❧

"What am I going to do about Vanessa?" Bruce asked Jenny. "Gramps isn't paying any more attention to her than he did to me when I first arrived. He doesn't get mad at her like he did with me; he just ignores her. She sits beside him while he watches television and greets him when he comes home after his golf game. She's doing everything she can, but he doesn't notice."

"Could you take her home with you?"

Bruce nodded. He'd been thinking about that.

"But you don't want to?"

He tried to explain how he felt. "Vanessa's a good dog, but she's not really mine, not like a pup would be."

"I got Schnoodle as a puppy. I trained her myself."

"Goldie and I were babies at the same time, but my mom says Goldie was lots easier to housebreak." Bruce laughed. "Guess I'll have to take Vanessa, if my folks will let me fly her home. Vanessa won't like spending hours in a crate with the baggage in the plane. But . . ."

"Maybe you should make one more try with your grandfather," Jenny suggested. "When he's in a really good mood, tell him that her owner has died. Maybe you can make it sound as if she just died. He'll be mad if he thinks you've been hiding that from him all these weeks. Get him in a good mood and then make him feel sorry for Vanessa. You can tell him that she is smart and well trained. If he'd walk her and take care of her, he might learn to like her. You could tell him that—if he was in a good mood."

"Do you know how to make mashed potatoes?"

Jenny looked confused. "What's that got to do with anything?" she asked.

"Gramps likes mashed potatoes. If I made him a special dinner—all the things he likes best—mashed potatoes and roast beef and blueberry pie . . ."

"Good thinking, Bruce!" Jenny punched him on the shoulder. "I'll help."

The next Monday, Gramps and Bruce went shopping. Gramps never cared what Bruce bought; he just paid for whatever was in the basket. On Tuesday morning Bruce said that he couldn't play golf with the Old Duffers. He had to rest up for his swimming lesson, he said, because Mac was going to time his speeds and rate his dives.

"That strikes me as harsh," Gramps said. "You're

supposed to be on vacation. Maybe I should talk with Mac. . . ."

"No," Bruce said quickly, crossing his fingers behind his back. "I want Mac to test me so I'll know just how good I am. Sometimes I think he tells me I'm better than I really am just so I'll feel good."

Gramps shrugged his shoulders, picked up his clubs and went out. Bruce sighed with relief and phoned Jenny.

By the time she arrived, he was already stirring water into the pie-crust mix. "Anyone who can read can cook, my mother says. She's right."

"Piece of cake," laughed Jenny.

"Piece of pie," Bruce corrected her.

That was *before* they rolled out the dough. "My mother does it like this." Jenny divided the dough into lumps and put one on the counter. Then she began to roll with the rolling pin. It stuck to the dough, and the dough stuck to the counter top. The more they rolled, the stickier it got.

Bruce fished the pie-crust-mix box out of the waste basket and read the directions again. "Flour. We're supposed to flour the rolling surface."

It took a long time to scrape all the sticky dough off the counter and back into the bowl. While Jenny shaped it into a ball again, Bruce spooned flour onto the counter. They put the dough on top of the flour and then more flour on top of the dough. Bruce began to roll.

"My mother's come out round," Jenny announced as she tore some of the dough off the long ragged edge and stuck it onto the skinny edge. Jenny rolled for a while, but the dough looked more like the map of the United States than a circle.

"We'll cut off the edges after we get it in the pan." Getting it in the pan was more difficult than either of them had imagined.

There were big tears in the edges and a bump in the middle. They pushed the bump down into the pan. There was no dough on one edge of the pan and dough hanging over the other edge.

"We'll just have to move Florida." Jenny pulled off a long skinny piece and pressed it on the side where the Great Lakes had been. Bruce ran a knife around the edge of the pie pan to cut off all the other ragged edges.

The filling was easy. All they had to do was open the can and pour the blue stuff in the pan. They rolled out the top crust, and it was almost the right size. And then they put the pie in the oven.

Flour and blobs of dough dotted the kitchen, even the floor all the way across the room from where they had been working. They had cleaned the counters and scrubbed the kitchen floor when they smelled something. Blue pie filling was dripping over the sides of the pan to the bottom of the oven. The crust was brown, maybe just a little too brown.

"Must be done," they said at the same time.

They took the pie to the den and put it on the desk on a magazine to hide it from Gramps. Then Jenny and Bruce stood back to admire it.

"Not bad," Bruce said.

"Piece of cake." Jenny left before Gramps got home from his game.

Bruce told Mac about the special dinner and about his lie to get Gramps to golf without him.

"I don't want you to be a liar," Mac said, and went back to the dressing room and returned with a stopwatch. "Stand here. When I say 'go,' make your best racing dive and swim your best four laps. I'll time you."

When Bruce finished the test, Mac said his time had been better than most of his best high-school freshmen could do.

Bruce cut his lesson short and rushed home to fix the dinner. First he took the roast beef out of its plastic wrapper and put it in a baking pan. Gram's cookbook said to preheat the oven to 500°. He did that. Then he began to peel the potatoes.

What was that terrible smell? It came from the oven. When he opened the oven door, smoke curled out. The drippings from the pie were burning. The smoke alarm began to beep.

"What's going on here?" Gramps stood looking down into the oven. "Something burned over? Never mind." He went to turn off the alarm, and Bruce put the roast in the oven and turned the heat down to 325°.

Gramps opened all of the windows and turned on the kitchen fan.

The doorbell rang. "It's nothing," Gramps said. "Just a little kitchen mishap. Two bachelors living here, you know." He laughed. "No, Mrs. Byrd, we don't need help. Thanks anyway."

Bruce finished peeling the potatoes and put them in a pan with lots of water, covered the pan and put it on the stove. Then he took the extra-special vegetables he had bought—something called the San Francisco mixture—from the freezer. The picture on the package made them look delicious. He emptied them into a pan and added butter and water according to the directions.

He made the salad. He had bought blue-cheese dressing—Gramps always ordered blue-cheese dressing when they ate out—to go with it. He set the table at the end of the living room.

It was going to be a terrific meal, and Gramps would be so happy. He began to compose his speech about Vanessa. First he would tell Gramps, straight out, that her owner had died. Then . . .

He tested the potatoes with a fork. They were soft, so he drained off all the water and poured milk into the pan. That's what Jenny had said to do. Then he got out the portable mixer and put it in the pan and turned it on. Milk and lumps of potatoes flew out of the pan onto the counter and the floor. He lifted the mixer and more lumps flew. He turned off the mixer.

Another strange smell. More smoke rising, from the pan with the vegetables. He turned off the heat and took the pan to the sink, skidding on spilled milk and potatoes as he rushed to get cold water into the vegetable pan.

Gramps took the pan out of his hand. "Can't eat that." He took it outside to the garbage.

Bruce wiped up the milk and potato lumps with a paper towel, and then he put the mixer back in the pan with the rest of the potatoes and turned it on very slowly. The potatoes crumbled and mixed with the milk and turned fluffy—just like Mom's. So they wouldn't have a vegetable; there were vegetables in the salad.

The timer buzzed; the roast was done. He took it from the oven.

"Looks delicious," Gramps said. "Want me to carve it?" He got out the carving knife and set the roast on a board and began to run his knife across the surface.

"Knife must be dull." He sharpened the knife and tested it with his finger and again applied it to the roast. "I can't imagine," he muttered as he pressed harder and harder, shaking his head.

Bruce stood watching; his stomach began to knot. While Gramps was still trying to cut off the first slice, Bruce went to the phone and called Jenny. The vegetables didn't matter, but they had to have meat.

Jenny asked her aunt, and came back to the phone. "She wants to know what kind of roast it is."

Bruce fished the wrapping out of the wastebasket. "It says 'chuck roast.' "

"Chuck roast," Jenny told her aunt, and then she groaned. "She says that's for pot roast. You have to cook it in a lot of liquid for a long time. She says the thing to do is to put it in a big casserole or a Dutch oven and pour water over it and put it back in the oven for another two hours. She says to add a package of onion soup if you've got any, or a cut up onion, or a can of tomato sauce or some catsup. She says it will be delicious."

"But the potatoes are done now. It's dinnertime." He hung up without saying good-bye. His stomach felt sick. He'd tried so hard. . . . "Wrong kind of roast." He tried to sound cheerful. "This is for pot roast."

"I like pot roast even better." Gramps got out a big black pot with a lid and put the roast in it.

Bruce found a box of onion-soup mix and sprinkled it over the meat. Then he squirted catsup on top of that while Gramps put water around it. They put it back in the oven.

"It won't be ready for two hours." Bruce was hungry—and very tired.

"The salad looks good," Gramps patted him on the shoulder. "What else is there?"

"Mashed potatoes. You like mashed potatoes." He lifted the lid and showed them to Gramps.

"Good. I've missed mashed potatoes. We'll have mashed potatoes and salad."

"And blueberry pie! Jenny and I made it." Bruce rushed to the den, suddenly happy. *Who needs meat when we have Gramps' favorites—mashed potatoes, salad with blue-cheese dressing and blueberry pie?*

He flung open the door to the den. There stood

Vanessa, her whiskers covered with blue—and an empty pie pan.

Bruce went crazy. "You dumb, stupid, ugly dog. This whole dinner was for you! Well, you can just go to the pound. No one will want to adopt a crazy dog like you. You'll be put to sleep, and I won't care."

Vanessa came and licked his hand, smearing it blue.

Bruce pushed her aside and ran to the bathroom and washed his hand. He never wanted to see blueberry-pie filling again. He didn't want to see Vanessa either. He sat down on the edge of the tub and did something he hadn't done since Goldie died. He cried.

❀ 9 ❀

After a while Gramps came and put his hands on Bruce's shoulders. "I really appreciate the dinner you tried to make, Bruce," he said softly. "I can see that it didn't come out quite as you planned, but it's the thought that counts. Now tell me about that dog. She surely doesn't have to go to the pound just because she ate a pie."

"Her owner is dead, Gramps. She died weeks ago, and I didn't tell—"

"I know." *How could he know?* "I read about her death in the Villa Verde paper. I assumed you were planning to take the dog home with you. I can understand that. She's a pleasant animal. Reminds me of a dog I had when I was a boy. His name was Blacky. He was the best friend I had when I was a boy on the farm."

"But you don't like Vanessa."

"What makes you think that? Actually, I've thought

some of buying a dog for myself since I've met Vanessa. This apartment will be empty again when you leave. No one to greet me when I come in. Just empty, silent spaces all around me."

"You *like* Vanessa? She was a good dog—until she ate our pie. She's already trained. Training a dog is a lot of work, you know. And she's settled. Puppies chew things and make messes. . . ."

"But you'd rather have a puppy?"

Bruce nodded. "I didn't think I'd ever want another dog after Goldie, but I'm beginning to change my mind."

"So let's make a deal. You give me Vanessa, and I'll give you the money to buy another golden retriever, if that's what you want."

"I don't know what I want. I thought I'd look first at the pound." Bruce couldn't believe Gramps. "You *really* want Vanessa? You never paid any attention to her."

"I tried not to notice her so I wouldn't get used to her and then miss her when she was gone. The apartment will be so lonely when you leave."

"Not with Vanessa here. She'll be at the door waiting for you when you come home from your golf games. That's one of the great things about dogs—they're always so glad to see you."

"So that's settled. She'll be my dog. That being the case, I'm going to make some changes. Her name, for one thing. Can you imagine me out walking a dog named Vanessa? When I was a boy, we gave dogs nice, simple names like Spot and Ace. I'll call her Van."

Bruce nodded. Van was a good name for a dog.

"And that silly-looking barrette has to go. Come, Van."

Van came leaping into the tiny bathroom and wedged herself between Gramps and Bruce.

"She has such a kindly face," Gramps said as he reached into a drawer and pulled out a pair of scissors. "Sit," he said to Van. "You hold her head," he said to Bruce.

Van sat, and Gramps cut the barrette out of her hair and dropped it into the wastebasket. Then he trimmed her topknot into a crew cut. When he was finished, Van looked different—not pretty, but not silly, either.

"There's my lovely little lady," Gramps cooed. Gramps cooed? It didn't seem possible.

Van licked his hand, and he reached down and scratched her crew cut. Then he washed the pie filling out of her whiskers.

"Come on. Let's eat." Gramps reheated the mashed potatoes and heaped them on plates with slices of ham that Bruce had bought for sandwiches. They had salad with blue-cheese dressing, and ice cream.

After dinner Gramps loaded the dishwasher and Bruce walked Van over to Jenny's.

"Is that you, Vanessa, with a new hairdo?" Jenny called as soon as she saw them. "Who is your barber?"

"My new master, Gramps," Bruce answered in his best barking voice. "But call me Van. My new master has changed my name."

As they walked the dogs, Bruce told Jenny about the burned vegetables and the pie that Van ate. "Everything went wrong. . . ."

"Except the important part. Vanessa has a home."

"While we were eating, Gramps said that Van likes to watch television with her head on his foot. He thinks that's clever."

"Schnoodle does that."

"So did Goldie."

Gramps walked Van every morning and afternoon. Bruce still ran her after dinner with Jenny and Ottie. The next time Mac asked about her, Bruce told him the whole truth. "Only thing is that her new owner is spoiling her just like her old owner did. He lets her sleep on the bed, and he feeds her from the table!"

Bruce would never feed his puppy from the table; he'd train him to sleep beside his bed, not on it. Bruce thought more and more about the puppy he might get.

The California bachelors played tennis and golf and chess. They watched games on television and went to a Dodgers game. They ate out often and took turns cooking when they ate at home. During the last week Gramps took Jenny and Bruce to Disneyland.

Whenever the Blue Funk tried to come back, Van would sit between Gramps and the television with her head resting on Gramps' knee. In a little while Gramps would get up and take Van for a walk. When he came back, the Blue Funk would be gone.

On the way to the airport Gramps made a speech: "You know, Bruce, I've been a very lucky man. Jane could have married anyone, but she didn't. She married me, and we had forty-two years together. I have all those forty-two years to remember, and I have my daughter and my grandchildren. God's been good." He reached over and patted Bruce's knee. "Thanks for coming, Bruce. And thanks for leaving Van. I hope you'll find another dog you can love almost as much as your Goldie. There'll never be another dog quite like your Goldie."

With his tennis racket on his shoulder and his flight bag in his hand, Bruce walked up the ramp to the plane. He turned once and waved to his Good Buddy, who was standing straight and smiling.

It had been a turnip summer for a few weeks, but in the end it had been as smooth as a milk shake. He was a good swimmer now, thanks to Mac. He was a better tennis player, thanks to Gramps. He had a new friend, Jenny. He'd send her a picture of his puppy. He'd probably name the puppy Milk Shake.